The Shape of my Heart

Mark Sperring

Illustrated by Alys Paterson

BLOOMSBURY

LONDON NEW DELHI NEW YORK SYDNEY

This is the shape of our eyes.

And these are the shapes we might see.

clink!

tick-tock!

raaaa!

crunch!

wibble-
wobble!

yummy!

splish-splash!

This is the shape of the sun,
coming up to brighten our day.

And these are the shapes that chirp and tweet...

chirp!

tweet!

flutter!

flitter!

chirp!

chirp!

tweet!

chirp!

tweet!

tweet!

flitter!

tweet!

flutter!

tweet!

and flitter-flutter away.

HELLO!

This is the shape of our mouths.

hello!

Hi!

hello!

HELLO!

hello!

hi!

Now, what would
you like to eat?

Something hot?

Or something
cold?

Something savoury?

Or sweet?

This is the
shape of my
shoes.

Aren't they nice?

And this
is the shape
of your feet.

brrrm!

brrrm!

And these are the shapes that pass us by…

beep!

beep!

chug!

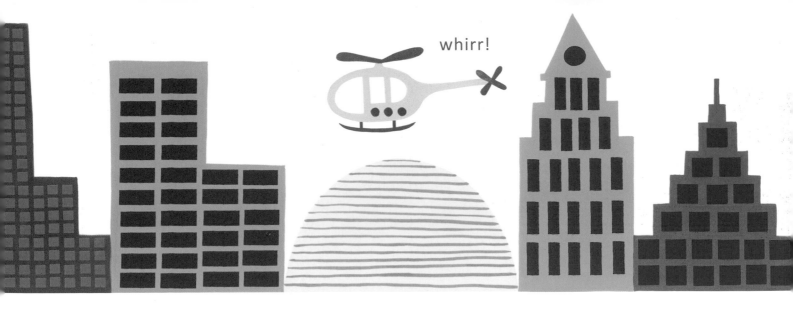

whirr!

beep!

beep!

on a noisy, busy street.

vroom!

vroom!

chug!

beep!

This is the shape of my hand.
The hand you hold on to.

Where are we going and what will we see?

roar!

Let's look at the
shapes at the zoo!

snap!

grrrr!

hisssss!

squeak!

owooo!

flap!
flap!

This is the shape I
hear you with.

Are you feeling sleepy?

LET'S BE ON OUR WAY!

And this is the shape we come back to . . .

at the very end of the day.

This is the shape of the pillow where you lay your sleepy head.

And this is the shape of the toy
that you cuddle up to in bed.

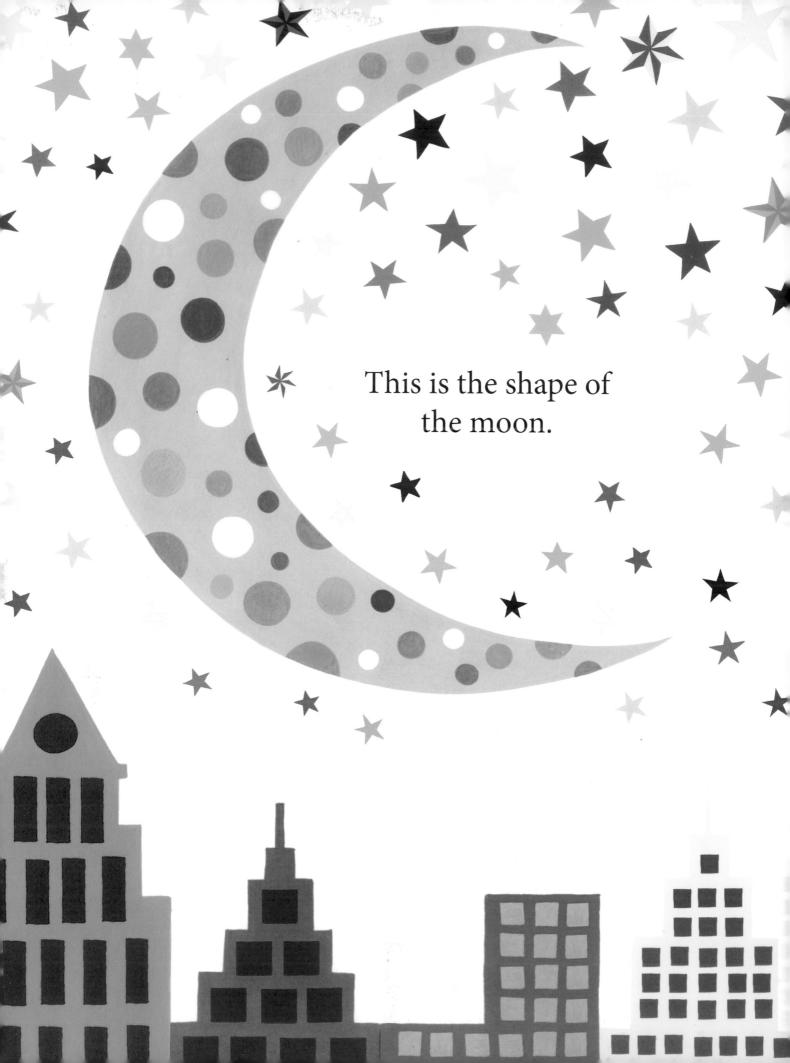

This is the shape of
the moon.

And these are the shapes
of the stars...

And this is the shape
I love you with.

This is the shape of
my heart.

For you . . . to read with those you love
~ MS

For Mum, Dad, Bob and Gran with all my love
~ AP

Bloomsbury Publishing, London, New Delhi, New York and Sydney

First published in Great Britain in 2013 by Bloomsbury Publishing Plc
50 Bedford Square, London, WC1B 3DP

Text copyright © Mark Sperring 2013
Illustrations copyright © Alys Paterson 2013
The moral rights of the author and illustrator have been asserted

A CIP catalogue record for this book is available from the British Library

ISBN 978 1 4088 2704 8 (HB)
ISBN 978 1 4088 2705 5 (PB)
ISBN 978 1 4088 4061 0 (eBook)

Printed in China

1 3 5 7 9 10 8 6 4 2

All papers used by Bloomsbury Publishing are natural, recyclable products made from
wood grown in well-managed forests. The manufacturing processes conform to the
environmental regulations of the country of origin